W9-ATY-687

By Lynn Hodges & Sue Buchanan

A Song of God's Love

Illustrated by John Bendall-Brunello

Count Yourself to Sleep

zonderkidz

zonder**kidz**®
The children's group
of Zondervan

www.zonderkidz.com

Count Yourself to Sleep
Copyright © 2005 by Lynn Hodges and Sue Buchanan
Illustrations © 2005 by John Bendall-Brunello

Requests for information should be addressed to:
Grand Rapids, Michigan 49530

Library of Congress Cataloging-in-Publication Data

Hodges, Lynn.
  Count yourself to sleep : a song of God's love / by Lynn Hodges and Sue
Buchanan ; illustrated by John Bendall Brunello.– 1st ed.
      p. cm.
  Summary: Rhyming text suggests taking time after saying prayers and good-
nights to count all of the "good and perfect gifts" that God has bestowed, such
as teddy bears, a warm bed, and a mother's kiss.
  ISBN 0-310-70717-X (hardcover)
  [1. Gratitude–Fiction. 2. Bedtime–Fiction. 3. Stories in rhyme.] I. Bendall-
Brunello, John, ill. II. Title.
  PZ8.3.H6655Cou 2005
  [E]–dc22

                                                            2004000283

All Scripture quotations unless otherwise noted are taken from the *Holy Bible: New
International Version*®. NIV®. Copyright © 1973, 1978, 1984 by International
Bible Society. Used by permission of Zondervan. All rights reserved.

All rights reserved. No part of this publication may be reproduced, stored in
a retrieval system, or transmitted in any form or by any means—electronic,
mechanical, photocopy, recording, or any other—except for brief quotations
in printed reviews, without the prior permission of the publisher.

Zonderkidz is a trademark of Zondervan.

Art direction & design: Jody Langley

Printed in China

05 06 07 08 09 /CTC/ 10 9 8 7 6 5 4 3 2 1

*Every good and perfect
gift is from God.*
—James 1:17

You're all cozy and cuddly
and comfy in bed.

We've hugged and we've kissed
and our prayers have been said.

But don't fall asleep yet,
you sleepyhead, you!

Let's play one more game.
Here's what you do.

Are you ready?

Count yourself to sleep!
Count yourself to sleep!

Before you wink, before you blink,
and think you're gonna nod,
count your good and perfect gifts.
They all come from God!

When you wake in the night,
and you're all by yourself,
what should you do?
Get the toys off the shelf?

Turn on the light?
Ask for a drink?

No! It's dark and it's quiet.
It's the best time to think.

I'll count myself to sleep!
I'll count myself to sleep!

3

4

2

1

0

Before I wink, before I blink
and think I'm gonna nod,
I'll count my good and perfect gifts.
They all come from God!

6

7

And all through your life,
from now till you're grown,
when you lie down at night
and feel sad and alone...

Count all the ways
God has shown you his love!
Ev'ry gift good and perfect
comes from above.

I'll count myself to sleep!
I'll count myself to sleep!

Before I wink, before I blink
and think I'm gonna nod,
I'll count my good and perfect gifts.
They all come from God!
I'll count my good and perfect gifts.
They all come from God!

Teddy bears with button eyes.
Chocolate pudding! Very nice!

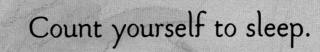

Count yourself to sleep.

Sunshine warm and flowers bright.
My warm bed, the dark of night.

Count yourself to sleep.

Frogs and turtles, worms that crawl.
Going swimming, playing ball.

Daddy's lap and Mother's kiss.
I think I'll dream of all this!
Count yourself to sleep.

Mom! Are you asleep?

Unbelievable!